Frieda B.™
Meets the Man in the Moon

by Renata Bowers
pictures by Michael Chesworth

To my parents, for your faith in my wings.
To Julie, for helping to seed and shape this story.
And to Michael Chesworth, for your incredible gift
and your sensitivity to the world of childhood.

ISBN 978-0-9843862-1-5

First Edition.
Library of Congress Control Number: 2012914879
Printed in the United States.

To visit Frieda and/or order additional
books from the Frieda B. series, go to
www.FriedaB.com.

Frieda B., Frieda B., on a warm night in June,
took a trip, took a trip, took a trip to the moon.
Took a trip to the moon, for she just had to know
what it's like where the rockets and astronauts go.

And so…

On that warm night in June, with the moon full and bright,
Frieda thought, "I must go, and I must go tonight.

For the moon's full and bright, so I'll see where I'm going.
I'd surely get lost with just half the moon showing."

She planned out her course and she picked out a bag
for her moonboots and helmet and polishing rag.

She tested her compass, then whistled for Zilla
who rushed in with ice cream – three pints of vanilla.

With everything packed, Frieda jumped on her bed,
    counted down ten to one, then yelled, "Watch out ahead!"

And before she could blink or think twice, they indeed
were careening through space at a bed-rattling speed.

Up ahead, what was once a small circle of moon
      was now growing in size, like a big white balloon.
And behind – way behind – in a faraway spot
      was the earth, which had shrunk to a blue and green dot.

"What a strange sight indeed," Frieda B. had to marvel.
"The earth is as small as a little blue marble.
Why Fiddle-Dee-Dee's just a tiny green speck,
and the farther I go, well, the tinier it gets."

As she stared at the earth, Frieda's bed went KA-BOOM!!
She'd watched earth for so long, she'd crashed into the moon.

"Goodness me!" exclaimed Frieda, her hair all a mess.
"Next time I should watch where I'm going, I guess."

As she gathered her things and got set to explore,
Frieda heard something moaning, then groaning some more.

"Where on earth is that coming from?" asked Frieda B.
Then a big booming voice said, as hurt as can be,
"It's not coming from earth, it is coming from ME."

Frieda ran to the edge of the moon and looked 'round.
    And she rubbed her eyes twice when she saw what she'd found:
a big mouth and big nose and two big, teary eyes –
    yes, The Man in the Moon, nearly ready to cry.

"My goodness," said Frieda, "What makes you so teary?
The Man in the Moon is supposed to be cheery."

"You'd be teary, too, yes you would be," he said,
"if a girl and her bed had crashed into your head.

Not only is what you've done downright unlawful,
  it's made a big mess and it hurts something awful."

As Frieda B. listened, she reached in her bag
    and she dried his big tears with her polishing rag.
"Mister Man in the Moon," Frieda said, "I feel awful
    for hurting your head and for being unlawful.

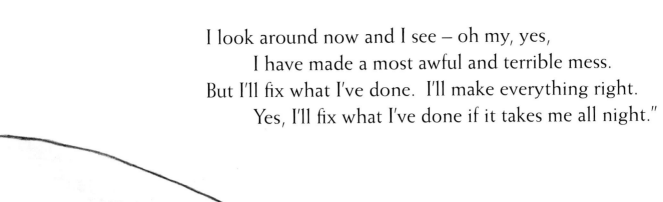

I look around now and I see – oh my, yes,
     I have made a most awful and terrible mess.
But I'll fix what I've done. I'll make everything right.
     Yes, I'll fix what I've done if it takes me all night."

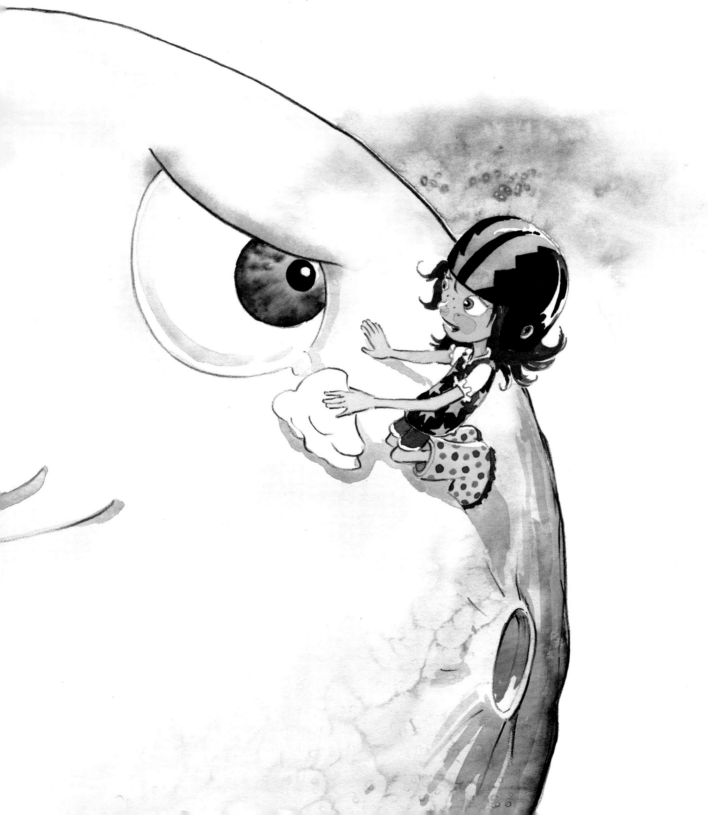

And so that's what she did. Frieda fixed every gash,
    every dent, every scrape that she'd caused with her crash.

She put everything back in its place. And then later,
she polished each rock and swept every last crater.

She cleaned so completely that when she was done,
The Man in the Moon beamed as bright as the sun.
"Frieda B.!" exclaimed he with a gleam in his eye,
"You have made me the happiest moon in the sky!"

So by keeping her word, Frieda B. made amends.
    And the two who'd been strangers became best of friends.

On the earth down below, people wondered that night
    how the moon had become so uncommonly bright.

They looked out their windows.
    They stared from their beds.
        They questioned their neighbors.

They scratched puzzled heads.

And while earth stared in wonder that warm night in June,
Frieda played hide-and-seek with The Man in the Moon.